138628
0.5pts.

# RAINFORESTS

Precious McKenzie

ROURKE
PUBLISHING

www.rourkepublishing.com

www.rourkepublishing.com

PHOTO CREDITS: Title Page: © Denali55; Page 4: © roccomontoya, © Jason Register; Page 5: © szefei; Page 6: © 3000ad; Page 7: © Alan Craft; Page 8: © labaaaato, © Tammy616; Page 9: © TommyIX; Page 10: © suc; Page 11: © rustyphil; Page 12: © Kitch Bain, © Jin Tat Teh; Page 13: © Eduardo Rivero; Page 14: © awilms, © olof can der steen, © andy2673; Page 15: © hotshotworldwide;Page 16: © Anneke Schram, © melusa2; Page 17: © shannonplummer; Page 18: © pixhook, © archives; Page 19: © mareenpr; Page 20: © luoman, © ricardoazoury; Page 21: © Antonio Oquias; Page 22: © Gualberto Becerra; Top Page Border: © PacoRomero; Bottom Page Border: © julos

Edited by Kelli L. Hicks

Cover Design by Nicola Stratford   bdpublishing.com
Interior Design by Renee Brady

**Library of Congress Cataloging-in-Publication Data**

McKenzie, Precious, 1975-
Rainforests / Precious McKenzie.
    p. cm. -- (Eye to eye with endangered habitats)
Includes bibliographical references and index.
ISBN 978-1-61590-316-0 (Hard Cover) (alk. paper)
ISBN 978-1-61590-555-3 (Soft Cover)
1. Rain forest ecology--Juvenile literature. 2. Rain forests--Juvenile literature. I. Title.
QH541.5.R27M427 2011
577.34--dc22
                        2010009857

Rourke Publishing
Printed in the United States of America, North Mankato, Minnesota
033010
033010LP

www.rourkepublishing.com - rourke@rourkepublishing.com
Post Office Box 643328  Vero Beach, Florida 32964

# Table of Contents

# What's So Special About Rainforests?

Found near the **equator**, rainforests are warm, extremely wet areas that have many trees. Rainforests receive 77 inches (200 centimeters) to 400 inches (1,000 centimeters) of rain annually. The average temperature in a rainforest is 90 degrees Fahrenheit (32 degrees Celsius).

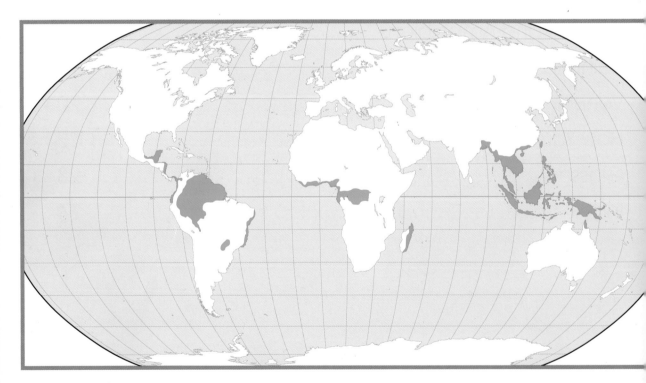

Areas that are rainforests.

Tropical rainforests, approximately 6% of Earth's surface, grow in Central and South America, Australia, Asia, and Africa.

# Where Does All of This Rain Come From?

Rainforests create their own rain. As the tropical Sun warms the rainforest in the morning, **mist** rises through the trees. This mist forms because of the moisture left on the plants combined with the extremely warm temperatures. Then, the mists rise and form clouds over the rainforest. Later in the afternoon, moisture-filled clouds pour rain down upon the forest. This cycle continues day after day in the rainforest.

*The clouds over the mountains in Ecuador, South America, play a vital role in the continuation of the rainforest water cycle.*

*Sometimes the mist forms so thick in → the rainforest it is nearly impossible to see very far in front of you.*

# Trees Like Skyscrapers!

The rainforest has many layers. The tallest trees form the emergent layer which is the top layer of the rainforest. The next layer is called the **canopy**. Trees in the canopy often grow more than 200 feet (61 meters) tall. The thick, green canopy shades the understory of the forest.

This rainforest canopy in Brazil acts like a ceiling hiding any animals beneath the thick layer of trees.

Some animals and insects that live on the rainforest floor will never reach the top of the rainforest canopy. They prefer a home where it is moist and dark.

Monkeys and → butterflies thrive in the towering emergent layer of the rainforest.

# Beneath the Canopy

The layer underneath the canopy is the understory and it is found above the rainforest floor. Flowers, butterflies, bats, and birds live in the dark, hot, understory.

The lowest layer, the shady forest floor, contains soil, dead leaves, water, and insects. More insects are found in rainforests than anywhere else on Earth.

*The rafflesia flower grows in Indonesian rainforests. This flower grows over 39 inches (100 centimeters) in diameter.*

*Moss and algae grow on moist* ➡️
*rocks on the rainforest floor.*

# Feathered Friends

A variety of birds live in rainforests. Macaws, conures, toucans, harpy eagles, hummingbirds, lorikeets, and hornbills thrive in the fruit and insect rich **environment**.

*The Sun Conure, belonging to the parrot family, is a loud member of the rainforest habitat.*

*The hornbill looks like a prehistoric creature that lives in southeast Asia and Africa. It eats insects, fruit, and small animals.*

*The bill of the Toco Toucan of South America grows →
up to seven and one half inches (19 centimeters)
long, but is surprisingly lightweight.*

# Rainforest Mammals

Rainforest **mammals** are an unusual group of creatures. Bats, sloths, and monkeys hide in the trees. Armadillos and anteaters feed off of the abundant insects. Tapirs, bandicoots, and coatis feed off plants, fruits, worms, and insects. Predators such as tigers, ocelots, jaguarundis, leopards, and jaguars dine on the abundance of smaller animals.

*An anteater's tongue stretches up to two feet (60 centimeters).*

*Ocelots are fantastic swimmers and stalk their prey at night.*

*Coatis are highly intelligent cousins to the raccoon and are no bigger than a pet cat.*

*The three toed sloth spends most of its life in the trees and sleeps for 18 hours per day!* ➡

# Reptiles and Amphibians

The warm, moist forest creates the perfect home for **amphibians** and **reptiles**. Anoles, poison dart frogs, boa constrictors, pythons, anacondas, flying dragons, chameleons, caimans, and crocodiles are just a few of the hundreds of reptiles and amphibians scientists identified that live in the rainforests of the world.

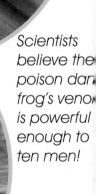

*Scientists believe the poison dart frog's venom is powerful enough to ten men!*

*Caimans are members of the crocodile family and are very dangerous, even though some people try to capture them as pets.*

*The Green Tree Python is an endangered* → *species because humans have hunted it for its skin, meat, and to sell as pets.*

# Rainforest Flora

The plants of the rainforest do not only feed and shelter animals, they feed people, too. Humans harvest cocoa, bananas, vanilla, avocados, coffee, mangoes, papayas, macadamia nuts, cashews, and Brazil nuts from the rainforests.

*We use vanilla beans in many of our favorite foods.*

Humans also make products out of rainforest plants. Rubber, chewing gum, rattan furniture, and bamboo flooring all come from plants found in the rainforest.

### Rainforest Fact:

Scientists use rainforest plants to develop new medicines for sick people. Quinine, the drug for **malaria**, and ipecac, the drug for **dysentery**, originates from plants. Researchers even think that the cure for cancer will come from rainforest plants.

*Sometimes the papaya is called the paw paw and is eaten in salads, stews, and made into juice.*

# Vanishing!

Conservationists estimate that forty to fifty million acres (twenty million hectacres) of rainforests are destroyed each year. Logging, mining, farming, and road construction cause most of the damage to this delicate **ecosystem**. If we humans do not change our practices, rainforests could completely vanish in less than one hundred years.

Large, barren tracts of land are all that remain of thousands of acres in the Amazon.

Loggers cut down trees that are over one hundred years old and rarely plant saplings to replace the old trees.

Loggers stack trees that have been cut down ➡ and burn them in order to clear land for farming.

# How You Can Help

To conserve existing rainforest land, you should purchase sustainable products. These are plants grown and harvested in a responsible manner by small family farmers who live near the rainforest.

You can educate others by telling them the importance of protecting rainforests. Write to conservation organizations, your state or local government representatives, and international corporations. Encourage them to work closely with other nations and businesses to protect rainforests.

Encourage people to plant trees, recycle, and shop responsibly. Some of the small decisions you make each and every day could have a profound impact on saving the world's rainforests.

# Glossary

**amphibians** (am-FIB-ee-uhnz): cold-blooded animals that live in water and breathe with gills when young and later developing lungs and living on land when mature

**canopy** (KAN-uh-pee): a cover over something

**dysentery** (DIS-uhn-ter-ee): a disease caused by bacteria or parasites that cause diarrhea, pain, and fever

**ecosystem** (EE-koh-siss-tuhm): a community of plants and animals

**environment** (en-VYE-ruhn-muhnt): land, sea, and air

**equator** (i-KWAY-tur): imaginary line around the center of the Earth

**malaria** (muh-LAIR-ee-uh): a tropical disease transmitted by mosquitoes that causes fever, chills, and sweating

**mammals** (MAM-ulz): warm-blooded animals that nurse their young

**mist** (MIST): a cloud of small water droplets found in the air

**reptiles** (REP-tilez): cold-blooded animals that live on dry land and lay eggs

# Index

# Websites to Visit

www.kids.nationalgeographic.com/Photos/Tropical-rainforests

www.kidsplanet.org/

www.nature.org/rainforests/explore/facts.html

# About the Author

Precious McKenzie was born in Ohio but has spent most of her life in south Florida. Her love of children and literature led her to earn degrees in education and English from the University of South Florida. She currently lives in Florida with her husband and three children. They try to do their part by recycling.